For Alan, who knows where to find the magic
—A. B. M.

For Alice, who has opened my eyes in so many ways
—A. B. H.

For F. B. & S. D. A., kindling my fascination with our beautiful, mysterious oceans
—S. L.

SIMON & SCHUSTER BOOKS FOR YOUNG READERS
An imprint of Simon & Schuster Children's Publishing Division
1230 Avenue of the Americas, New York, New York 10020
Text copyright © 2020 by Alice McGinty and Alan Havis
Illustrations copyright © 2020 by Stephanie Laberis
SIMON & SCHUSTER BOOKS FOR YOUNG READERS is a trademark of Simon & Schuster, Inc.
For information about special discounts for bulk purchases, please contact Simon & Schuster Special Sales at 1-866-506-1949 or business@simonandschuster.com.
The Simon & Schuster Speakers Bureau can bring authors to your live event. For more information or to book an event, contact the Simon & Schuster Speakers Bureau at 1-866-248-3049 or visit our website at www.simonspeakers.com.
Book design by Krista Vossen
The text for this book was set in Edlund.
The illustrations for this book were digitally rendered.
Manufactured in China
0220 SCP
First Edition
2 4 6 8 10 9 7 5 3 1
Library of Congress Cataloging-in-Publication Data
Names: McGinty, Alice B., 1963- author. | Havis, Alan B., author. | Laberis, Steph, illustrator.
Title: The sea knows / Alice B. McGinty and Alan B. Havis ; illustrated by Stephanie Laberis.
Description: First Edition. | New York : Simon & Schuster Books for Young Readers, 2020. | Text is presented in rhyming verse.
| Audience: Ages: 4–8 years. | Audience: Grades: 4–6.
Identifiers: LCCN 2019028096 (print) | ISBN 9781534438224 (Hardcover Picture Book) | ISBN 9781534438231 (eBook)
Subjects: LCSH: Ocean—Juvenile literature. | Oceanography—Juvenile literature. | Deep-sea ecology. | Deep-sea animals—Juvenile literature.
| Hydrology. | Natural disasters—Juvenile literature. | Rhyme. | Illustrated children's books.
Classification: LCC GC21.5 .M391886 2020 (print) | LCC GC21.5 (eBook) | DDC 551.46—dc23
LC record available at https://lccn.loc.gov/2019028096

The SEA KNOWS

Alice B. McGinty &
Alan B. Havis

Illustrated by
Stephanie Laberis

A PAULA WISEMAN BOOK
Simon & Schuster Books for Young Readers
New York · London · Toronto · Sydney · New Delhi

We are young.
The sea is old.

The sea has secrets
to unfold.

The sea knows.

The sea knows huge.

The sea knows small.

The sea knows tall.

The sea knows short.

The sea knows spots,

the sea knows shiny.

The sea knows smooth,

the sea knows spiny.

The sea knows strong,

the sea knows weak.

The sea knows hide.

The sea knows seek.

The sea knows stars
in shallow pools.

Below, it knows
alluring jewels.

The sea knows worlds
of red and gold.

The sea knows bright.

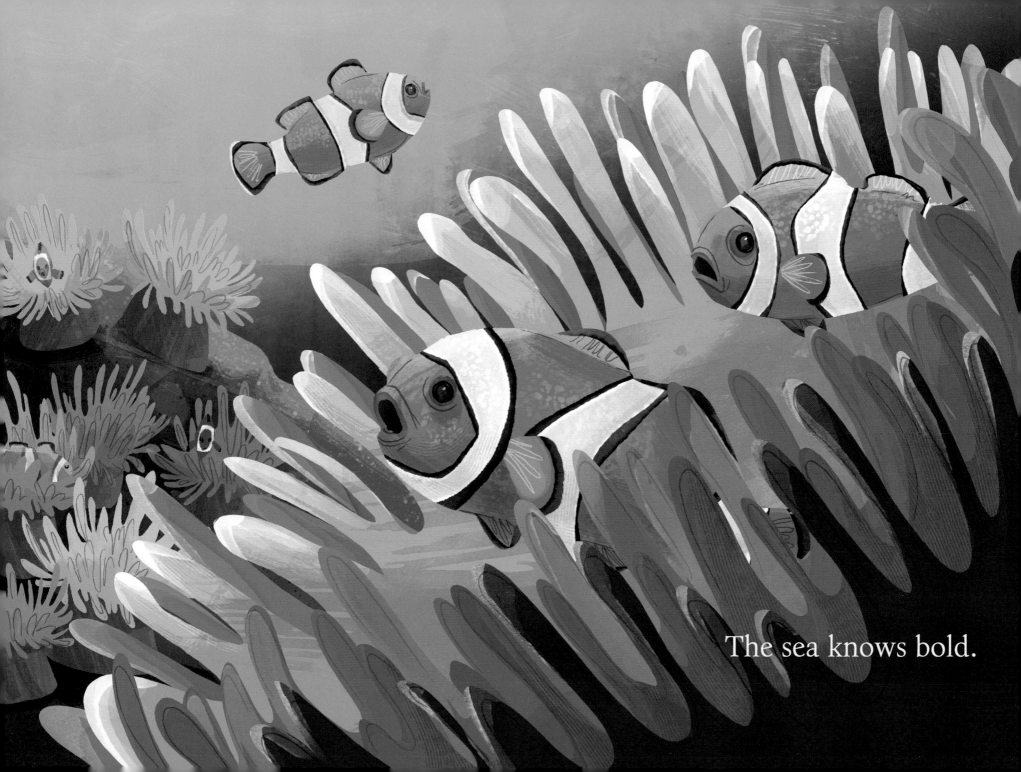

The sea knows bold.

The sea knows white,

and orange, too.

The sea knows silver,

and green,

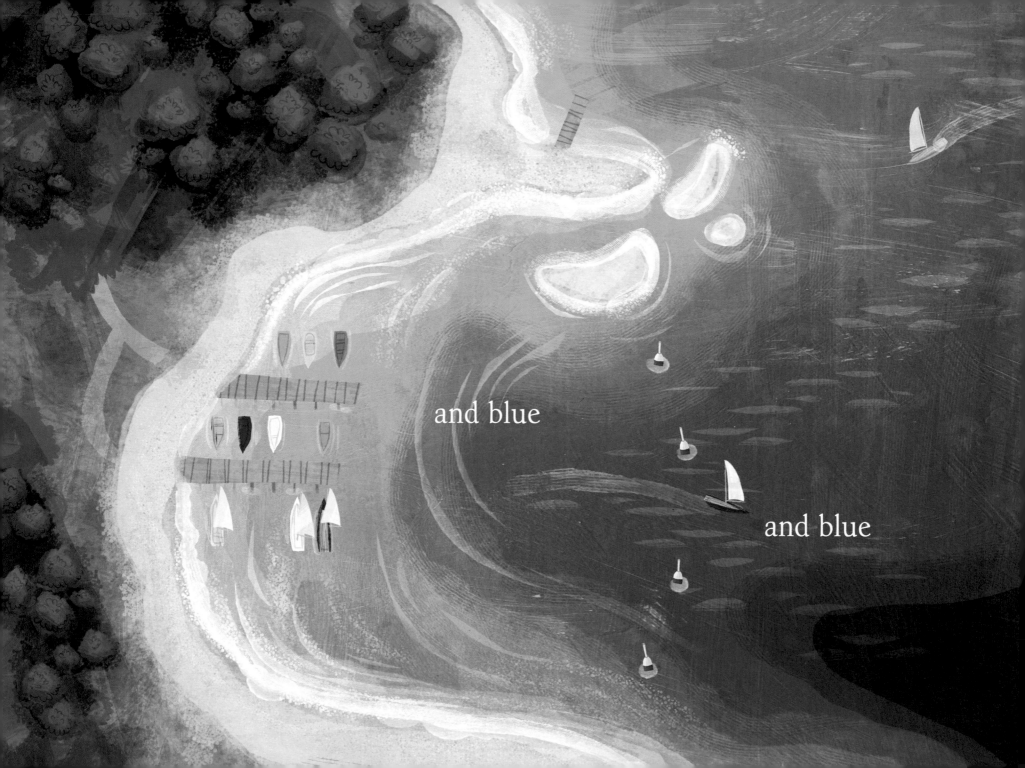

and blue

and blue

and blue.

The sea knows depths as black as ink.

The sea knows float.

The sea knows sink.

The sea knows splash,

the sea knows bubble.

The sea knows crash.

The sea knows trouble.

The sea knows wind,

and waves that tower.

The sea knows storm.

The sea knows power.

The sea knows when
the storms should cease.

The sea knows calm.

The sea knows peace.

More About What the Sea Knows

The sea knows huge.

The sea is home to the hugest creature on earth—the blue whale—which grows to around one hundred feet long, nearly the length of seven cars lined up end to end.

The sea knows small.

Did you know that the biggest sea creature, the blue whale, eats some of the smallest? Krill are tiny shrimp-like animals that are only between a quarter of an inch and two inches long. There are so many krill in the sea, it is estimated that combined they weigh more than all the humans on earth.

The sea knows short.

Flat-topped crabs are so short, they look as if they've been squashed. These tiny creatures are not much more than a quarter of an inch tall!

The sea knows tall.

If you took a blue whale and stood it on its tail, it would be less than half as tall as giant kelp, the largest kind of seaweed, which can grow up to 215 feet high. They form huge, thick forests where many sea creatures hide.

The sea knows spots.

When predators see the bright color and black spots of the yellow boxfish, they know to stay away. These fish release poison into the water when they think danger is near. Bright colors and spots warn predators, "Stay clear. I'm dangerous!"

The sea knows shiny.

There are many shiny fish in the sea. Their silvery skin acts like a mirror, reflecting light to help the fish blend in with the color of the water so they can't be seen by predators.

The sea knows smooth.

Have you ever felt the inside of a shell? It's made of a very smooth, hard substance called mother-of-pearl, which protects the soft creature inside the shell. After the sea creature dies, people may find the shell and use mother-of-pearl to make jewelry.

The sea knows spiny.

The puffer fish's long spines lie flat against its body . . . until the puffer fish senses danger. Then it sucks in water, inflates its body up to three times its size, and—poof!—its sharp spines shoot straight up!

The sea knows strong.

Piranhas are strong, especially when it comes to biting. Piranhas have the strongest bite relative to their body size of any fish—three times stronger than an alligator of the same size!

The sea knows weak.

Piranhas eat many weak, tiny fish that live in the sea. The weak have their ways to survive, though. They swim in bunches, sometimes by the thousands, and the group moves quickly, changing direction all at once, so it's hard to catch them as they zip through the water.

The sea knows hide.

Sea creatures are experts at hiding! Some, such as octopi, squid, and cuttlefish, can instantly change their color and texture to match the background where they hide. Hey . . . where'd that octopus go?

The sea knows seek.

Sharks are the ultimate predators and they use their sharp senses to search for prey. Their keen sense of smell detects even a tiny amount of blood in the water. They listen for splashing sounds. And their eyes are on the lookout for the flickering shapes of fish's shiny scales.

The sea knows stars in shallow pools.

Starfish (or sea stars, as scientists call them) suction themselves to the ocean floor with rows of tiny tubes on their undersides. There are close to two thousand kinds of starfish in all sizes, shapes, and colors. While most starfish have five arms, some, such as sun stars, have up to forty arms!

Below, it knows alluring jewels.

Down deep, the sea is so dark that the only way to be seen is by turning on a light. That's what the anglerfish does. The female anglerfish has a spine that sticks out from above her mouth, like a fishing pole, with a light at the end. When other fish see the shining light and swim toward it, the anglerfish opens her big mouth and gulps them down.

The sea knows worlds of red and gold.

This red and gold coral is part of a coral reef, built from the shells of many tiny coral that lived before. Even though coral reefs cover a small area of the ocean, they are home to almost a quarter of the creatures in the sea.

Coral reefs are threatened by natural and man-made causes. Scientists have developed ways of restoring damaged reefs by growing or reattaching coral, but there is still much work to be done. People as young as sixteen can volunteer to help.

The sea knows bright.

In the luminescent comb jelly, bright colors and light come together to make a swimming light show. The cilia, or hairs, on the creature's sides wave as the creature moves through the water, scattering light, which causes the color show.

The sea knows bold.

The clownfish boldly lives within the poisonous tentacles of the sea anemone. Don't worry. A special coating on its body protects the clownfish. The sea anemone provides safety, and in return the clownfish helps the anemone. Small fish, attracted to the clownfish's bold colors, swim right into the anemone's tentacles. Lunch!

The sea knows white,

Nudibranchs are sea slugs, and they come in many stunning colors, including bright white. The long offshoots on the sea slug's body are called cerata. The cerata help the creature absorb oxygen from the water.

and orange, too.

This dazzling orange sea sponge, along with the many other ocean sponges, is among the simplest kind of animal in the sea. Sponges have no organs in their bodies. They are simple collections of cells which take in food from the water passing through them.

The sea knows silver,

Vast schools of herring zip and flash through the water like a mass of shooting silver stars. There can be hundreds of millions of them in just one school! There are more herring than almost any other kind of fish in the sea, and they provide food not only for people, but for millions of bigger fish.

and green,

There is a lot of green in the sea, including thousands of kinds of green algae. Green algae can be dark green or light green. It can be short and fuzzy, or long and wavy—and everything in between.

and blue and blue and blue.

When you look at the sea, you find many shades of blue. Why does the sea's clear water look blue? Water absorbs most colors of the sun's rays, but blue light is scattered instead of absorbed, so we can see it. The deeper the sea is, the darker the blue looks. That's because in deep water the sun's rays don't reflect off the sea floor.

The sea knows depths as black as ink.

The deepest sea is more than 35,000 feet deep. That's so deep, if Mount Everest rose from the bottom it would still be more than a mile underwater! When you go deeper than 4,000 feet, the sea is totally dark, and the only light is from glowing sea creatures. Over 90 percent of the ocean's water lies in total darkness.

The sea knows float. The sea knows sink.

Everything is made of tiny pieces. How tightly those pieces are packed together determines density. Things that are denser than the water sink. Things less dense than water float. Air is less dense than water. Ships float because they are hollow and filled with air. If the ship fills with water, it sinks.

Even the sea itself can float. When water freezes it becomes less dense. That's why ice floats.

The sea knows splash.

When humpback whales smack their tails on the surface of the water, they make a huge splash. One reason the whales splash is to scare fish into swimming below them, so the whales can dive to eat the fish.

The sea knows bubble.

Humpback whales use bubbles to catch their prey. One whale releases air from its blowhole beneath the surface to make a huge "net" of bubbles. The other whales circle around the fish, forcing them into the "bubble net." Then the whales swim up through the bubbles, eating the fish.

The sea knows crash. The sea knows trouble.

A lot of crashing goes on in the sea. Waves crash onto the shore, and sometimes ships crash too. There are a huge number of shipwrecks in the sea. It is estimated that there are more artifacts and pieces of history on the ocean floor than there are in all the museums in the world.

The sea knows wind,

The sea plays a big part in making wind. How? The air over land is warmed by the sun. As it warms, it rises and cooler air from the sea moves in to fill its place. When the air moves from the sea to the land, it makes wind.

and waves that tower.

While the sea makes wind, the wind in turn makes waves. When wind blows against the surface of the sea, it pushes the water and makes it move, creating waves. Waves can be tiny or huge. The tallest wave ever measured was near Alaska. It was 1,719 feet tall. That's more than a quarter mile high and taller than the Empire State Building!

The sea knows storm.

The sea knows many kinds of storms, from huge thunderstorms to wild hurricanes. Just as warm air rises to make wind, storms are created when warm, wet air rises from the sea's surface. As the air gets higher, it cools and forms clouds and rain.

Hurricanes are the most violent storms of all, with strong winds swirling at seventy-four miles per hour or more. They form over tropical seas where the air is very warm.

The sea knows power.

From howling hurricanes to the towering waves of tsunamis, the sea knows power! Tsunamis are caused by underwater earthquakes. The earthquake creates a wave, which travels at about five hundred miles per hour. As it comes toward the shore, it builds into a powerful, destructive wave up to a hundred feet high.

People are trying to harness the power of sea currents and waves to make electricity. There is enough energy in the seas around the United States to power almost two times the number of homes in the U.S.